NORWOOD HOUSE PRESS

Oh! Ani...

By Kathleen Corrigan

Search for Sounds
Short vowels:
o, u

Scan this code to access the Teacher's Notes for this series or visit
www.norwoodhousepress.com/decodables

DEAR CAREGIVER, *The Decodables* series contains books following a systematic, cumulative phonics scope and sequence aligned with the science of reading. Each book in the *Search for Sounds* series allows its reader to apply their phonemic awareness and phonics knowledge in engaging and relatable texts. The keywords within each text have been carefully selected to allow readers to identify pictures beginning with sounds and letters they have been explicitly taught.

When reading these books with your child, encourage them to isolate the beginning sound in the keywords, find the corresponding picture, and identify the letter that makes the beginning sound by pointing to the letter placed in the corner of each page. Rereading the texts multiple times will allow your child the opportunity to build their letter sound fluency, a skill necessary for decoding.

You can be confident you are providing your child with opportunities to build their foundational decoding abilities which will encourage their independence as they become lifelong readers.

Happy Reading!

Emily Nudds, M.S. Ed Literacy
Literacy Consultant

HOW TO USE THIS BOOK

Read this text with your child as they engage with each page. Then, read each keyword and ask them to isolate the beginning sound before finding the corresponding picture in the illustration. Encourage finding and pointing to the corresponding letter in the corner of the page. Additional reinforcement activities can be found in the Teacher's Notes.

Oh! Animals
o, u

Pages 2 and 3	Have you ever seen an octopus? They are amazing animals. They live underwater in the ocean. An octopus has eight long arms. It also has big bulgy eyes and a round body. An octopus swims backwards. It can also crawl on the bottom of the ocean, looking for food. An octopus often swims up and then down in the water. It can be upside down or right side up.
	An octopus likes to eat other ocean animals like shrimp and lobster. It uses the suction circles on its arms to pull the food to its mouth.
	An octopus can change its color. When it is on top of some sand or a rock, it can change color so it is camouflaged.
	How does an octopus keep track of all its arms? Just imagine putting an undershirt on eight arms!

Keywords: gull, lobster, octopus, rock, undershirt, underwater

Pages 4 and 5	Ostriches are huge birds. They are taller than a man. They are odd birds because they can't fly, but they can run very fast. Ostriches also have strong legs and claws. An ostrich can kick hard enough to hurt a lion!

Ostriches are huge birds. They are taller than a man. They are odd birds because they can't fly, but they can run very fast. Ostriches also have strong legs and claws. An ostrich can kick hard enough to hurt a lion!

They live in dry grassy places in Africa with lions, cheetahs, African wild dogs, giraffes, zebras, and other animals.

A mother ostrich lays her eggs in a hole in the ground after it is dug by the father ostrich. The mother sits on the eggs all day waiting for the eggs to hatch. The father sits on the eggs all night.

When the chicks hatch, they stay with their mom and dad. Sometimes ostrich parents make shade with their wings to keep their babies out of the rain or hot sun.

Sometimes an ostrich will lie on the ground to hide. It stretches its long neck and lies still. Its feathers match the sandy ground so it is hard to see.

Keywords: dogs, hot, log, mom, ostrich

Read this text with your child as they engage with each page. Then, read each keyword and ask them to isolate the beginning sound before finding the corresponding picture in the illustration. Encourage finding and pointing to the corresponding letter in the corner of the page. Additional reinforcement activities can be found in the Teacher's Notes.

u

Pages 6 and 7	An umbrellabird is a bird that lives in the rainforest. They are mostly black, but some have red feathers, too. They have a feather tuft on top of their heads that looks like an umbrella. Some people think the tuft of feathers is funny.
	Umbrellabird moms make nests for their eggs. The nests are high up in the tree to keep the eggs safe.
	Umbrellabirds are big birds and they can't fly very far. They often hop between branches. When they sleep, they look like black mops. Their heads are under their umbrella feathers and their feet are under their wings.

Keywords: bug, mud, sun, tuft, umbrella, umbrellabird

o, u

Page 8	Otters are cute animals. There are different kinds of otters. Some live by lakes and rivers. Some live in the ocean.
	River otters can run on land and swim in the water. They have their babies in dens under the ground. The pups stay in the den until they learn to swim and hunt. Sometimes the mother will push a pup into the water to give him a swimming lesson.
	River otters like to play with each other. They play in the snow, splash water, and wrestle on land and in the water.

Keywords: mom, otters, pup, under

o, u

Page 9

Sea otters are much bigger than river otters. They float on the ocean waves in groups. Mother otters raise their pups without the father helping. The pup will often lie on mom's chest and tummy to sleep or snuggle.

Sea otters go under the water to hunt for food like crabs, snails, and clams. After it catches the food, the otter will lie on its back and use its chest like a table.

Keywords: mom, otter, pup, snuggle, tummy

o, u

Pages 10 and 11

Oxen are cattle that are taught to do work. They pull plows or lug big loads.

An ox learns to wear a yoke. It is made of wood and sometimes leather. The yoke goes under the ox's neck and on its shoulders. The ox owner puts the yoke on the ox when it is time to work and takes it off when the ox is finished working. The owner can hang it up for the next time.

The owner teaches the ox a few words. When the person says "whoa," the ox will stop.

Oxen often work together. Two oxen will share a big yoke. This helps them move together.

People take good care of their oxen. They feed them and brush them and let them out in the field to graze and rest.

Keywords: jug, ox, oxen, pull, sun

Norwood House Press • www.norwoodhousepress.com
The Decodables ©2024 by Norwood House Press. All Rights Reserved.
Printed in the United States of America.
367N—082023

Library of Congress Cataloging-in-Publication Data has been filed and is available at
https://lccn.loc.gov/2023024975

Literacy Consultant: Emily Nudds, M.S.Ed Literacy
Editorial and Production Development and Management: Focus Strategic Communications
Inc. Editors: Christine Gaba, Christi Davis-Martell
Illustration Credit: Mark Harmon
Covers: Shutterstock, Macrovector

Hardcover ISBN: 978-1-68450-720-7   Paperback ISBN: 978-1-68404-866-3
eBook ISBN: 978-1-68404-925-7